FIRROSE

Susan Jeschke

FIREROSE

Holt, Rinehart and Winston
New York Chicago San Francisco

In warm memory of Ida Virnick

Published simultaneously in Canada by
Holt, Rinehart and Winston of Canada, Limited.

A Holt Reinforced Edition

Printed in the United States of America
Designed by Jack Jaget
Published, March, 1974
Second Printing, February, 1975

Library of Congress Cataloging in Publication Data
Jeschke, Susan.
Firerose.
SUMMARY: Zora, the fortune teller, doesn't know
what to do when she finds a fire-breathing baby with
a curly green tail on the doorstep.
[1. Dragons–Stories] I. Title.
PZ7.J553Fi [Fic] 73-12515
ISBN 0-03-011991-X

ZORA, the fortuneteller, sat at her window watching the street. Mike, her cat, watched with her. Mike was a magic cat who could grow small and large at will. People with problems came to Zora for advice. And with Mike's help she was able to advise them. The clients would go away well pleased. And Zora would reward Mike with fish cakes and kidney and lung pies.

One evening there was a loud knock at the door. "Come in," Zora said, thinking it was a client. Zora opened the door and looked out. No one. Then she saw, lying in a basket at her feet—a baby!

"Agh—a problem," she said. She brought the basket into the house. Zora tickled the baby's stomach, and the baby smiled. The baby was a little girl—but not an ordinary little girl. This one had a delicately curled green tail.

"Agh—a problem," said Zora. She gave the baby a bath and put her to bed.

That night Zora stayed up late thinking. A little girl with a tail was a real problem. Mike nibbled a fish cake and sighed. "Well, my Mike, what should be done?" she asked.

"Ask Lucia," Mike answered.

The next morning Zora summoned her friend Lucia. Lucia was in the same business as Zora. She made little powders and liquids for her clients. Magical words and animal spirits were her specialty. She looked at the baby. "A beautiful baby!" she exclaimed, sighing over her and pinching the tail. "Now about this tail—" she said. She opened her handbag and took out her crystal ball. "It

says here that you must make the baby *like* her tail," she said. She looked at the baby again. "What is her name?"

The baby sneezed, and a little flame leaped from her nose. "She is sweet like a rose, she has a prickly stem, and she breathes fire. I'll call her Firerose!" Zora announced.

They all exchanged kisses and had tea to celebrate the name.

Zora and Mike grew to love Firerose, and Firerose loved them. But when Zora made clothes for Firerose, she saw to it that they covered up the tail. And she continually searched ancient books for ways to get rid of a tail. She hung garlic on it, hoping that it would be gone in the morning. On nights of the full moon she would chant a few words and rub half a potato on it, burying the other half of the potato in the ground (a remedy from Lucia). But the tail did not go away. Mike watched and said nothing.

One day Zora noticed that Firerose cried whenever her tail was touched

and that she breathed fire. Zora became worried. "What's the matter, Mike —is my Firerose sick?" she asked.

Mike looked at her coldly. "You are not doing what the crystal ball advised," he said. "How will she ever learn to like her tail if you keep covering it up—or trying to magic it away?"

Zora nodded. That evening she made Mike an extra-large fish cake, and a catnip meringue pie for dessert. "What can I do to make Firerose better?" she asked.

Mike banged his paw on the table. "No more spells, and no more hiding her tail!" he said. "Make her *like* her tail."

The next morning Zora went to the library and took out books with pictures of all creatures with tails. She covered the walls with kangaroos, horses,

lizards, devils, cats, dragons, monkeys and dinosaurs. Firerose liked the pictures. She began to stand in front of the mirror admiring her tail. Mike

showed her how to use it. Firerose discovered that she could swat flies—and hang from the fire escape upside down.

She especially loved to swim. She found that with a slight curve of her tail she could zip from one end of the tub to the other.

One summer day Zora, Firerose, and Lucia went to the beach. They found the warmest part of the beach and spread out a towel. Lucia sighed a sigh of

contentment. But before Zora could sit down she was dragged into the water by Firerose. "You stay near me, you hear?" Zora said sternly.

"This is even better than the bathtub," said Firerose, pulling Zora by the hand. Firerose swam farther and farther out, dragging Zora along. *Ouff!* . . . they hit a rock. A large rock. A large slippery rock that . . . had eyes and . . . great sharp teeth in the middle of a huge smile.

"Some problem!" Zora cried, pulling Firerose close to her.

The shark backed up, the better to view his dinner.

"Please, mister," Zora cried, "don't eat her—eat me. I'm bigger and I'd be much more filling."

The shark smiled, displaying a row of perfect teeth. "Well, O.K.," he said, and opened his jaws wide.

Zora gave Firerose a quick kiss, then thrust her out of the way. "Hurry! Go to Lucia——"

"He *can't* eat you, Zora—I won't let him!" Firerose cried. Like lightning, Firerose hissed a stream of fire, then whirled around and banged the shark on the nose with her tail. *Wap! Wap! Wap!* In a daze the shark swam off, not understanding what had happened to his dinner.

Zora took Firerose in her arms and kissed her. "You have saved my life," she kept repeating all the way back to the towel . . . all the way home on the subway . . . all the way back to the apartment.

Zora was filled with pride over her Firerose. She boasted to everybody about her wonderful child. At every opportunity she planted kisses on Firerose's nose.

When Firerose was five years old, Zora took her to school. The teacher looked down and said, "I'm sorry. This is a school for little children . . . not uh . . . hm . . . little dragons."

"Agh—a problem," Zora thought. She tried to explain how wonderful Firerose was; how because of her tail she had saved a life; how smart she was—but it was no use. The teacher refused to listen. Zora and Firerose walked home in silence.

Mike greeted them at the door. "Well?"

Zora told him all that had happened. That night, when Firerose was asleep, Zora sat at her table thinking. Firerose must go to school. "What can I do, Mike?" she asked.

"Ask Lucia," he said.

The following morning they told Lucia what the teacher had said. Lucia looked into her crystal ball. "At the same moment that Firerose was born," she said, "a dragon was born without a tail. You and Firerose must go to Dragon City to return the tail. A train leaves at midnight. Firerose will have no trouble getting into Dragon City. She is one of them."

"And me?" Zora asked.

"Don't worry. They will let you in too because of your love for Firerose," said Lucia.

Mike kissed them good-by and wished them luck.

The station was empty.

At midnight there was a quiet *whishsh* —like a fast whisper —and a train pulled up in front of them. Soon they were speeding away. Zora and Firerose could not take their eyes off the other passengers.

The train came to a halt and everybody got out. "Is this Dragon City?" Zora asked.

"Yes, it is," one of the dragons answered politely. The dragon directed Zora and Firerose to the king dragon, who kept records of the births of all dragons.

"Your dragonship," Zora began, and explained her reason for being there.

The king had no record of a five-year-old tailless dragon. "You will have to find him yourself. Our records aren't perfect."

"Agh—a problem," sighed Zora.

"It's all right, Zora," Firerose said. "If we don't find the dragon, I'll just keep my tail."

Zora sat down on a bench to rest, and Firerose ran off to play. A group of young dragons were playing ball. "Can I play?" Firerose asked.

"Yeah—you can take Izo's place."

Firerose flexed her tail and joined in the game. After a while she heard a loud sobbing. "What's that?" she asked.

"That's Izo—crying because he can't play."

"Why can't he play?" Firerose asked.

"Because he has no tail."

There on a bench sat a very sad dragon. "You're Izo?"

"Yes," he answered.

"Why are you crying?"

"They won't let me play because I have no tail," he sniffed.

"Look," said Firerose, "I have a beautiful tail." She switched it back and forth. "Would you like to have it?"

"Oh, yes!" Izo answered.

Firerose hugged him, took his hand, and raced off to Zora. "Zora, this is Izo. He has no tail, and he wants mine." Zora clapped her hands with joy.

Back they went to the king, who directed them to the dragon doctor. A large, friendly-faced dragon came out of his office. "I see . . . I see . . . this will not take long." Noticing the frightened expressions on Firerose's and Izo's faces, he added, "And it will not hurt."

Zora stayed in the waiting room. In a few moments the door opened and Firerose and Izo came out, Izo walking ahead switching his new tail proudly back and forth. "I hope you will be happy with my tail, Izo," Firerose said. "It looks very nice on you."

"But, Firerose, what will you do without one?" Izo asked.

"Oh, now that I'm a person, I don't really need one."

"It's time to go," Zora announced. Firerose and Izo bade each other good-by, and Izo said that if ever Firerose needed anything from him, she had only to ask, and that she was welcome in Dragon City anytime, even though she was a—person.

On the train ride back, Firerose wondered about her flame. Had that gone too? She breathed on the window. No flame; just mist. With her finger she drew a tail in the mist. Firerose looked sad. "I miss my tail, Zora."

Zora stroked her head, and Firerose soon fell asleep. How to make her happy without a tail?

Agh—a new problem.

She sighed.

Susan Jeschke

She was born in Cleveland, Ohio and presently lives in a storefront in Brooklyn, New York, which doubles as her studio. She is the author and illustrator of the popular picture book, *Firerose.*

About FIREROSE

*"One of the freshest, most imaginative books to appear lately." —*The Booklist*

"A lovingly illustrated story." —*Saturday Review*

*"A wonderfully down-to-earth fantasy." —*School Library Journal*